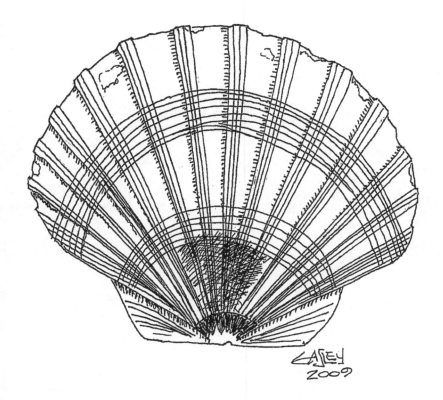

# Songs I Would Have Sung, Letters I Would Have Written, Dreams I Now Have Realized

## A Memoir of Pregnancy Loss, Adoption, and Birth

## Jayne H. Easley

iUniverse, Inc.

New York   Bloomington

**Songs I Would Have Sung, Letters I Would Have Written, Dreams I Now Have Realized**
**A Memoir of Pregnancy Loss, Adoption, and Birth**

iUniverse books may be ordered through booksellers or by contacting:

iUniverse
1663 Liberty Drive
Bloomington, IN 47403
www.iuniverse.com
1-800-Authors (1-800-288-4677)

Because of the dynamic nature of the Internet, any Web addresses or links contained in this book may have changed since publication and may no longer be valid. The views expressed in this work are solely those of the author and do not necessarily reflect the views of the publisher, and the publisher hereby disclaims any responsibility for them.

Illustrations © by Bruce W. Easley

ISBN: 978-1-4401-9142-8 (sc)
ISBN: 978-1-4401-9144-2 (dj)
ISBN: 978-1-4401-9143-5 (ebk)

Printed in the United States of America

iUniverse rev. date: 12/14/2009

Life is a flame that is always burning itself out,
but it catches fire again every time a child is born.
**George Bernard Shaw**

To Bruce, Mike, and Eric, the loves of my life—I am so grateful for each of you.

To my family and friends with loving appreciation for helping to get us through the dark and empty nights—it made all the difference.

To Roger, Dan, and staff—our immeasurable thanks and enduring affection for walking the difficult journey with us and for making the victories possible.

To the children we have lost, until we meet again ... loving each of you.

# Table of Contents

# Prologue

There are approximately six million pregnancies in the United States each year. Of these, nearly one third are lost at all stages of gestation and for a wide variety of reasons (American Pregnancy Association, 2009). While these statistics reflect the quantifiable reality of the events, they don't begin to address the grief, pain, and loss that accompany each occurrence.

Most of us assume that things will go according to our plan. If we put our minds to a purpose and carry out the necessary steps, we'll land that job, take that trip, or get pregnant pretty much on our predetermined schedule. It's a jolt to discover you're the exception to the rule, that the plans you made took a different course, and were not at all what you expected. Yet, as is so often the case in looking back from the distance of time or place or circumstance, something in that change brings new promise and a different insight, perhaps completely unlike the original blueprint, but extraordinary in its own right. This was our journey toward parenthood, but before I give the mistaken impression that the pitfalls weren't devastating or the losses not profound, I ask that you walk the miles with us. From there, you can draw your own conclusions.

My goal in writing this memoir is to share our journey and in doing so, provide a measure of hope in the face of extraordinary loss. If, through reading our story, we can give comfort to one couple or offer the promise of a dream realized to a single individual, then every moment spent putting the experiences to paper will be exceptionally worthwhile.

The American Pregnancy Association
United States Department of Health and Human Services
1425 Greenway Drive Irving, Texas 75038

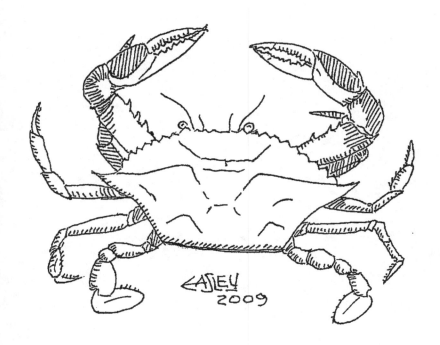

# Chapter 1
## The Beginning

I was twenty-six when I met Bruce on a blind date, and I was certain it was destined for failure. I'd had my share of friends trying to find my soul mate, and the results had typically been as far from anything soulful as it gets. This time though, despite my continued expressions of hesitation and anxiety about how the inevitable bomb might affect our friendship, I reluctantly agreed to a set-up with the uncle of my matchmaker friend's husband! Just trying to figure out the relationship was challenging enough, especially since the uncle I was about to meet happened to be younger than the nephew was!

As hackneyed as it sounds, I truly fell almost instantly in love with Bruce. He was nothing like I'd expected and everything I could have wanted. We had a fantastic time on that first date talking for hours over dinner in a quiet seafood restaurant. We never looked back from that point, and on May 20, 1978, a year and a half after our initial blind date, we were married, outdoors in a wonderful spot on the water. With the seventies drawing to a close, the Vietnam War finally over, and Fleetwood Mac's *Rumours* winning Album of the Year, our journey had begun.

The first year of our life together was typical of most newlyweds. We moved into a great home on a creek, settled into a routine, and looked to the future. We had decided to give ourselves a year before I got pregnant, just to enjoy this time, and become accustomed to our new lives together. We had already sewn our proverbial wild oats, lived independently, and were reasonably successful in our respective careers before getting married. So when the end of that first year came and we decided to take the giant step into parenthood, we assumed it would happen quickly as it had for all of our friends. Two months passed then five, then seven. When we'd tried unsuccessfully for a year, we decided to find out if there was a problem and if so, what we could do to fix it.

EASLEY
2009

# Chapter 2
## The First Stage of the Odyssey

A good friend at work had suggested her ob-gyn to me. The doctor was young and had a great new practice with another physician. Even though it meant traveling to the next town, some twenty minutes north, I decided to take Katy's recommendation. It was the beginning of our relationship with Dr. Roger Jones, the physician who would become our guide, our friend, and our hope.

In that initial meeting, Roger talked with Bruce and me about infertility and the various strategies that existed to bring about a successful pregnancy. He scheduled us for the first battery of tests and arranged for us to meet with him again once we had gathered all the data. We completed the questionnaires and exams and awaited the conclusions with considerable anticipation. As it turned out, we were both in good physical condition to achieve conception, but could probably benefit from a little extra help.

Anyone who has ever participated in the fertility dance is well aware of the physical and mental machinations required to fulfill the regimen. The thermometer, the alarm clock, the calendar, the casting aside of spontaneity (and often, passion), the contortions, the hope, and so often the disappointment, are all ingredients in an effort to determine the exact time of ovulation and thus, optimal fertility. I suspect it is one of the rare times in a man's life when sex isn't all it's cracked up to be!

Pharmaceuticals have come a long, long way in the many years since Bruce and I began our odyssey. In those days, we didn't have the product sophistication to pinpoint when I was ovulating, or was close to my period, or especially whether or not with virtual certainty, we'd been successful in conceiving. For several cycles, we participated in the fertility marathon, hoping at the end of each that this would be the one. For many agonizing months, it was not.

After repeated failure in this regimen, Roger decided it was time to bring in chemical reinforcements. I began taking Clomid, a fertility drug that helped to regulate ovulation and by extension, greatly enhance the chances of getting pregnant. The drug must have been the missing ingredient, because in just a few months, the magic happened. At long last, that little tadpole-looking guy found his eagerly waiting egg of a gal and the two became one!

Finally, after gymnastics, thermometers, and the help of a little white pill, we found ourselves expecting our first child. Our excitement was infectious. Family and friends knew how much we wanted this baby and how long we'd tried to conceive. This would indeed be one very welcome addition to our lives—the long awaited start of our family.

My pregnancy was fantastic. I felt great, never had the first moment of morning sickness, and carried on with my typically active life. In those early months, there were all the extraordinary milestones: the first time we heard the swooshing sound of the baby's heartbeat, the kicks that visibly moved my growing stomach, and the indiscernible sonogram views that looked more like amorphous JELL-O than human form. I had the usual obstetrical routine: monthly visits and exams and the standard questions about how things were going. Every indication pointed to an unremarkable pregnancy headed to a successful outcome.

\* \* \*

CASEY
2009

Reality sometimes has a way of grabbing you by the throat and often when you least expect it. Many years later, a beloved cousin would tell me shortly after the premature death of her husband that, "Things change in an instant." I didn't know then how true that was; I had not been so cruelly tested yet, but we would soon discover the unbearable impact of that reality. Almost imperceptibly, I realized an absence of activity. I was in the beginning of my ninth month and had become accustomed to the baby's frequent reminders that he or she was a presence that before long would make a wondrous, long-anticipated entrance. On many occasions, Bruce and I, like so many couples awaiting the birth of their child, would just lie on the bed watching and feeling the baby's kicks. It was comforting and reassuring—an unmistakable statement of fact that our little one was alive and thriving with a voice all his or her own—until the voice became silent.

I kept telling myself everything was okay. Maybe the baby had just gotten to the size that in the limited space, made moving a difficult challenge. When I called Roger to tell him about the changes I was experiencing, I was told he was out of town, but his partner, Dr. Dan Jenkins, whom I'd met on many occasions throughout the course of the pregnancy, would see me that afternoon. Bruce would come up right after work to meet me at the doctor's office.

There are those moments in life that we never forget no matter how many years pass or how much happens beyond them. Dan's face when he held the stethoscope on my now very large belly spoke, in silence, the thunderous reality that there was no heartbeat. Our baby was dead before there was ever a chance at life. In that instant, our dream came to a crushing, unthinkable halt. It was one of those terrible junctures when time stops and movement stalls as though slogging through a foot of snow. The situation is framed in a kind of surreal border that has no escape, yet cannot possibly be happening.

When Bruce came into the examination room, it was obvious that he knew, as well. Holding each other to cry was all either of us could express at that moment. We clung to one another as if in trying to absorb the other's anguish it might be diminished for both of us—it was not.

Clearly, it had not been any easier for Dan. It initially fell to him to confirm the reality to Bruce and me, and then to undertake the terrible task of relating to us what had to come next. I was scheduled for delivery the following morning, and it would take place in an examining room where a labor-inducing drug would be administered. Bruce would be by my side through it all. Dan would inform Roger of what had happened and ultimately relay to all of us the cause of our baby's death. The office staff would make arrangements with a funeral home of our choosing. Obviously, we were not the first couple to experience this agony, and we wouldn't be the last.

Our hearts were broken, our bodies ached from lack of sleep and hours of crying, our minds struggled without success to make sense of the terrible circumstance we were now facing. The morning of January 23, 1981, dawned cold but sunny and we had a terrible journey to travel.

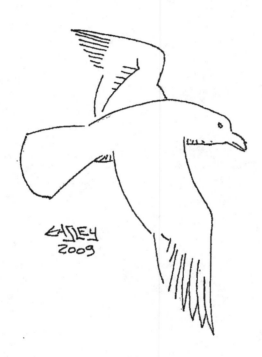

# Chapter 3
# Facing the Sorrow Together

The memories of certain events in our lives seem to have no discernible beginning and no definitive end. In the span between the emptiness of the confirmation of our baby's death and his ultimate entrance into the world, there was an intertwined series of prescribed events. Medical preparations were made, and together, Bruce, I, Dan, and Cathy, the OB nurse, reached the moment of delivery.

In looking back, I realize much more completely than I did then, that it was a time of incomprehensible contradictions: the first time we saw and held our son would be our last. The extraordinary anticipation of seeing his face, learning his gender, and substantiating the milestones of the past several months would be replaced with only the memories of his coloring, his personhood, his connection to us. The experience that should have been one of the most profoundly joyous of our lives was indescribably sorrowful. Our beautiful little boy emerged with the umbilical cord, the conduit of life, wrapped around his neck five times. Though he was perfect in every way, the lifeline between us had been the cause of his death.

From a scientific standpoint, there was little that the medical community could give us in the way of answers to the host of whys we expressed. It was a fluke of nature, a terrible event that just happened for no discernable or acceptable reason. From the far clearer vantage points of time and circumstance, I have come to feel differently about the nebulous basis for what happened, but more about that later.

The genuine sorrow and sympathy expressed by Dan, Roger, Cathy, and the entire office staff, meant a great deal to us. It marked the beginning of a long, caring, but tumultuous journey that would span a decade of heartbreak and joy.

We decided to pay tribute to our son and our brief time with him by spreading his ashes in a much-cherished point of land near the creek behind our home. Our family and friends honored his memory with us and we are certain, held their own children a little closer after sharing our loss that day.

I guess we all tend to venerate the extraordinary events in our lives with our own hallmarks, whether real or perceived. For me it came when, as we spread our baby's ashes and spoke a few words of love and farewell, a solitary seagull flew overhead. Even now, after all these years, whenever I'm at that point of land near the creek, I look for a gull and find great comfort when one happens to fly overhead. There were other healing steps as well. To this day, so very many years later, I still have the baby blanket that a dear friend had made for him and the knit cap that would have kept his head warm at birth. In our son's honor, Bruce and I planted a dogwood in the backyard and I've saved in a small basket with blue ribbon trim, all the cards and letters lovingly sent to comfort us. These mementos and tributes truly helped to get us through the days and nights of profound sorrow and immeasurable emptiness.

I don't know how I would have faced our loss without Bruce's love and support and that of our families and friends. To carry a child within you, regardless of how short or how extended the time, creates a bond of life and dreams that is unlike any other. Pregnancy loss is very broad in its reach, crossing lines of both present and future, affecting roles that were actually realized and those that were greatly anticipated. It is, arguably, a particular and cruelly unique bereavement that when apprised by those who have never known it, seems comparatively easy to overcome. Trite affirmations that assure there will be other opportunities, or that it's nature's way of protecting both parent and child from a lifetime of disability, or that thankfully, the child was taken before it was ever known, while statements of intended comfort, serve only to enhance the sense of isolation and misunderstood grief.

CASLEY
2009

# Chapter 4
# Moving Forward

We made the decision early on in our grief to follow the medically prescribed three-month waiting period and begin to try again. This time, I started taking the Clomid as soon as the effort to conceive began anew. However, getting pregnant before with fertility medication, and returning to the same regimen within a comparatively brief lapse of time, did little to speed up the process. I didn't get pregnant again until the following February. This would make my due date sometime around Thanksgiving—a very fitting holiday—and for me, a much-needed sign that things would fare significantly better this time.

As with our first pregnancy, the initial several months were uneventful. I felt great, had no morning sickness, and looked forward to the successful outcome that had so painfully eluded us in the past. I was on the regular monthly office visit regimen and the baby was growing and progressing as expected. During that time, my best friend's father was very ill and ultimately lost his life to a brain tumor. I got the okay from Roger, my physician, and flew to Maine to be with her and the family for the funeral. While in Maine, and on many other occasions during the first and second trimesters of the pregnancy, there were no indications of any problems, and Bruce and I began to give ourselves tentative permission to relax just a little, but the nemesis was not to be stilled.

At the start of my seventh month and without warning, my water broke. Frightened and fearing the worst, I called Roger and went to his office immediately. He discovered that the membrane had indeed ruptured, but sufficient fluid remained in the womb. The baby had not been compromised, but I would spend the next several weeks in very limited activity until we could reach a stage of confident viability: preferably, no less than thirty-six weeks. The gap between that goal and the present twenty-four weeks felt extremely daunting, but we had no choice, and any effort was worth enduring to have a positive outcome.

Despite reassurances and inactivity, the anxiety was almost overwhelming. This couldn't be happening again, especially when we all believed the first loss was a fluke. Time began to move at a sluggish pace on those long, quiet days, but we were grateful for the successful passage of each one and the chance to move another small step closer to having a healthy baby. One week passed, then three, and then, another month was behind us.

On October 27, a much-loved relative came by and offered to cook his special scallops in wine dinner for us. We were grateful for his company, the prospect of a terrific meal, and a break in the all-too-familiar daily routine. The evening went well, and we all enjoyed ourselves. It wasn't until late into the night that the problems began. I awoke feeling sick to my stomach. Whether it was due to the rapid race to the bathroom, the forceful reaction of vomiting, or just another horrific time of reckoning, I began to experience contractions. Bruce called Roger and we were directed to come to the hospital right away. I was twenty-eight weeks pregnant and a long, long way from the thirty-six weeks we had all been aiming for.

When we arrived, I was in full labor, and there was no stopping the momentum. It was also determined that the baby was in a breech position. For this reason and more significantly, due to the loss we had endured nineteen months earlier, it was felt it would be best if we delivered at the Medical College of Virginia. MCV was a renowned teaching hospital in Richmond. The neonatal intensive care facilities and innovative medical expertise seemed the best course to take. The decision was made to perform a cerclage prior to the trip, essentially stitching my cervix closed. I was carried by ambulance, and Bruce followed behind in our vehicle on the more than seventy-mile journey north; each of us hoping that the outcome would be far better this time.

Because of the baby's breech position, the delivery was by Cesarean section. I remember feeling as if I was about to be crucified when both of my arms were spread out on the surgical table and numerous lines, needles, and instruments were attached in one location or another. Bruce was by my side and shared each step of the process with me. Dan, who was on call that evening, had accompanied us, and he participated in the delivery along with Dr. Dwight Kruikshank of MCV.

The sensation of experiencing activity and movement in my stomach, but not actually feeling any pain, was unlike anything I'd ever encountered. Finally, the baby was born—a tiny, beautiful baby girl. Bruce was able to cut the umbilical cord, but then she was rushed to the neonatal intensive care unit (NICU) because of her considerable prematurity. We were reassured that despite her size, she seemed to be doing well and was receiving the best of care. We decided to name her "Suzanne Natalie" after my sister and my mother. There weren't any words to express our incredible mixture of feelings, running that very broad spectrum between fear and joy; or our overwhelming gratitude that our baby, although premature, had been delivered successfully and seemed to be doing well.

The next several hours were spent calling family and friends to share our wonderful news. While we were undeniably aware that the baby was facing difficult risks, I believe both Bruce and I had decided in an unspoken alliance to trust that she was going to be fine and that the profound sorrow at the loss of our son had now been vanquished. All those close to us shared our happiness and optimism, no one wanted to broach any other possibility.

We were able to see our baby in the NICU and although very small, she was perfect. Just being with her, even briefly, reinforced our belief that she would be fine. Bruce remained with me through the night. At daybreak, he decided to drive home, shower, change clothes, and pick up some items for me. He'd been gone for only about an hour when the phone by my bed rang. It was a nurse in the NICU informing me that the baby had suddenly taken a turn for the worse. Her condition was grave, and the unit was sending someone to bring me to her.

It has always amazed me how a dormant part of ourselves seems to come alive and kick into action in moments of crisis. For it surely wasn't me alone who had the presence of mind to call Bruce as my heart slammed against my chest, and the words I had just heard hung incomprehensibly in broken fragments in my head, but I did make the call. My husband assured me that he would return right away and that our love would get us through whatever we faced next.

There are snatches of memory in all of our lives that remain clear and unbroken by time. The gravity or the consequence, the extraordinary happiness or profound sorrow carve them into our psyche and cause them to become as much a part of who we are as any appendage. What occurred next is one of those memories for me. I can reconstruct virtually every moment of the following hours as easily as if they had occurred yesterday.

I was wheeled to the neonatal intensive care wing. The unit seemed especially far from my room this time, and the minutes required to travel the floors and halls that separated our daughter from me seemed endless. I could only imagine what an agonizing ride it would be for Bruce. Our home was more than seventy miles away from the hospital, and I knew he, like me, would be running every imaginable negative scenario through his head as he raced to get to us. When the doors to the unit pushed open, I vividly remember hearing a relentless and unbroken sound. I didn't realize it at that moment, but it was the heart monitor attached to our baby girl—the unmistakable, unceasing signal that I had arrived just as her life had ended.

If the constant humming of the machine had not given me the message, the looks on the faces of the nurses attending the baby would have. Their sadness and sympathy were unmistakable, and I remember feeling grateful for their initially unspoken sorrow. One of the nurses very gently removed all the wires from her little body, lifted our baby girl from the incubator, and handed her to me. We were taken to a nearby room to be alone together and to wait for Bruce to join us.

I will always remember him opening the swinging double doors to the unit and walking toward me as I held her in my arms. No words preceded his embrace, but his face spoke a thousand messages of anguish and loss. There is something soul rending about watching a man you love deeply—your father, your husband, a brother, a friend—cry body-shaking sobs that come from somewhere deep within that was almost always kept fortified and hidden. There was little to say to each other in that unforgettable moment. Together, Bruce and I, and yet another lost child, said good-bye in unquenchable sorrow and a wrenching disbelief that this was happening again.

I had to remain at MCV for a few extra days to recover from the surgery, while Bruce embarked on yet another sorrowful journey. The hospital reluctantly agreed to allow him to carry our baby daughter to the funeral home. He would relay to me many years later what an immeasurably sad and painful drive it was, alone for the last time with our lost child.

We decided to keep our farewell quiet and private. We again spread our baby's ashes at the point alongside her brother's. It was a place we would always cherish and where we could come whenever we wanted to spend quiet moments with the children we had lost.

# Chapter 5
## Continuing the Journey

Because lightning did strike twice in the same place, our physician felt strongly that we needed to investigate further, to determine if there was some other factor that was at the base of the problems we'd had, something that might have been missed. Roger scheduled me for a series of tests to be carried out a few months after the delivery to allow for some healing and recuperation for all of us.

In the meantime—partly as a diversion and partly to focus on the future—we decided to put an addition on the house. We did much of the work ourselves, completing a six-hundred-square-foot extension to the back of our home that greatly enlarged the kitchen and created a new family room. It really was therapeutic, if stressful in its own right. It gave Bruce and me a chance to spend a great deal of time together and to work through where we had been and where we hoped to go from this point.

I began diagnostic testing after the holidays. A series of different investigative assessments were completed, and then we met with Roger in late January to discuss the findings and consider the alternatives.

I have always been extraordinarily fortunate in my physical health and relative strength. My medical history had consisted of having my tonsils removed when I was nine, I experienced a mild case of pneumonia at thirteen, and had a benign cyst removed when I was in college. So when Roger relayed to us that I had a bicornuate uterus, a congenital defect that essentially created a dividing wall down the middle of my womb, I was stunned.

However, whether it made scientific sense or not, it explained to us in concrete, understandable terms why our son may not have had enough room in utero to avoid the strangulating cord that had entangled itself around his neck, and why our daughter was born too soon, when the pressure of her growing size forced the rupture of the membranes that protected her. For me, the diagnosis revealed another unshakeable reality: something inside of me was killing our children.

Clearly, that perspective was neither healthy nor completely accurate, but it plagued me then and does so to this day. Roger, with great care, made every effort to counter my thoughts with facts and statistics. He reassured me that it was one of those accidents of nature beyond anyone's control, and would not have been suspected without the kind of trauma we had undergone in our two failed pregnancies. The positive news was that the problem could be surgically corrected, and we were very fortunate to have one of the world's foremost obstetrical authorities in practice just a short distance away: Dr. Howard Jones, co-founder, along with his wife, Dr. Georgiana Jones, of the Jones Institute for Reproductive Medicine. Arrangements were made for him to perform the surgery, and Roger would participate in the procedure. This new phase of our journey would take place in February.

Dr. Jones was a very warm, reassuring physician, and despite world prominence in the field of in vitro fertilization, he was both humble and accessible. He carefully explained the defect and the process that would be undertaken to correct it. He relayed to Bruce and I that we would have to wait at least a year before attempting to get pregnant again. Dr. Jones also shared with us that like any surgical intervention, the procedure was not without risks or possible side effects, including a potential weakening of my already compromised cervix, as well as the typical concerns associated with infection and the use of anesthesia. Despite these possibilities and the required pregnancy delay, we were ready to move forward with hope, and defeat the elusive enemy that had been the source of so much sorrow and loss.

EASLEY
2009

# Chapter 6
# A Renewed Sense of Hope

In medical parlance, the surgery was a success. Everything went according to plan, and after several days of hospitalization and a few weeks of recovery, I was able to return to work. In the months that followed, we got together with Roger to discuss when we wanted to pursue attempting to get pregnant once again. We conveyed that we did want to try again, and when the prescribed year had passed, we began the fertility drug regimen. Surprisingly, I got pregnant almost immediately and this time, because of the surgery and the sense that we had a much better chance of success, we were able to feel some of the confidence that comes with experiencing a normal pregnancy.

The first trimester passed without incident. I was monitored on a regular basis, and because things were going well, I had gotten Roger's okay to travel home to Maine to visit my parents.

Very early one morning, I awoke to find I'd started bleeding. The old panic I'd known so well, returned; only this time, both Bruce and Roger were a thousand miles away. My parents rushed me to the hospital, and I met with a well-respected local ob-gyn. I relayed my history to him and he contacted Roger. I remained in the hospital for a couple of days and was ultimately released. The cause of the bleeding couldn't be pinpointed, and there didn't appear to be any apparent problem with the baby or threat to the pregnancy, but my old companion—fear—had returned and would stay with me for the duration; of that, I was certain.

The next three months passed without a problem or a crisis. The bleeding didn't recur, and we let our guard down just a little. That was our mistake. In mid-April, the seventh month of my pregnancy, without warning or apparent cause, my water broke.

Once again, Bruce and I, in the wrenching drill we had marched too often in the past, rushed to Roger's office. After he examined me, he confirmed that I was indeed in full labor, and while steps would be taken to delay or stop it, there were no guarantees that any measures would work. In addition, Roger felt it best if I again went by ambulance to the Medical College of Virginia to an obstetrician specializing in high-risk births. Once more, he felt that the chances for the pregnancy, and ultimately the baby, would be better at MCV. The arrangements were completed and with Bruce by my side, we made the agonizing journey, traveling once more the seventy-plus miles north to Richmond.

When I arrived at MCV, the physician with whom Roger had consulted was temporarily unavailable. Unfortunately, we had apparently come at a chaotic time. The hospital was short staffed and several obstetrical emergencies were occurring simultaneously. I was taken to a room where Bruce and I remained without contact with any medical personnel except for a very young nurse assistant. When Bruce asked about the physician we were supposed to see, we were told he was involved with another emergency and would get to us as soon as possible. Sadly, little babies—especially those in crisis—don't follow our time frames or the dictates of the outside world.

As Bruce and I waited in the room with the assistant standing at the foot of the bed, I felt an uncontrollable thrust. I was mortified. I cried out thinking I had just had a bowel movement. I remember the look of fear on the young woman's face as Bruce squeezed my hand and told me as calmly as he could, that I had just delivered the baby—a tiny little girl. He yelled to the very frightened aide to get help, and in what seemed like an eternity, nurses arrived, cut the umbilical cord, and swept the baby away to the neonatal intensive care unit.

This nightmare wasn't happening again, not in this place, not after all that had happened to change the outcome. Not when we were supposed to be in a state-of-the-art hospital, and not when we thought we had bested the nemeses that had defeated us twice before. Surely, this could not possibly be, but it was, and the ending was to be the same as well.

The baby did not survive the night. She weighed one pound, fourteen ounces and died of respiratory distress syndrome, an affliction that affects the lungs of premature babies. In reality, the technical name and cause didn't matter. We had lost our third child despite our belief that we had overcome the reasons for the previous losses and our certainty that we would never again have to experience this profound sorrow.

We were in a strange place with no vehicle, broken spirits, and our dead baby. We called our best friends and asked if they could come and get us. Maybe it seems unfathomable to some, but on the long, heartbreaking drive back home, together with Donna and Butch, Bruce and I held our little girl in the backseat of the car carrying her home for the first and last time.

How could this have happened again? What twisted scheme of fate could create the same unthinkable end with an entirely new set of circumstances? We had followed all the rules and taken no unnecessary chances. We had embraced the suggested procedures and were given assurances that the barriers that had created the previous losses were successfully addressed and removed. We felt ravaged and defeated, fighting an enemy that had no face or substance, yet conquered us anyway. We were trapped in a terrible medical cycle. There seemed to be no reconciling the experience we had just lived through.

This time, the agony came despite extraordinary strategies to prevent it. This time, in spite of an emergency placement in a large teaching hospital equipped to confront any challenge with renowned expertise and sophisticated technology, no one but a young nurse's aide was present. This time, in the face of great encouragement, medical affirmations, and extraordinary steps, we couldn't stop the terrible reiteration that had clearly become our unwanted destiny.

In medical terms, the loss was the result of an incompetent cervix, possibly exacerbated by the reconstructive uterine surgery. In human terms, it seemed a cruel joke, an unimaginable twist of circumstances that turned cure into culprit and remedy into tragic repetition. The sense that there indeed was something within me that continually killed our babies was inescapable now, and the agony of that unfathomable dichotomy of roles was at times overwhelming. The journey toward reconciliation would be even more difficult with this loss, and in no small measure, worsened by the increasingly inescapable indication that my bearing children might well be impossible.

Not long after losing the baby, I remember meeting a coworker. She offered her condolences and was certainly genuine in her expressions, but her parting words conveyed perhaps the starkest example I'd had of well-meaning statements cutting like an unforgiving laser. She told me the reason I hadn't had success thus far was that I hadn't prayed hard enough. She spoke that statement to me more than twenty-five years ago. It was extremely painful to hear then and remains so to this day.

I realize it was expressed with positive intention and certainly not meant to cause pain, but I mention it because it is glaring in its insensitivity and unfathomable in its judgmental nature. It is, as well, not atypical of the kinds of statements one is likely to hear with pregnancy loss. It's as though it is a grief in exile, a loss before attainment, a good-bye before the first hello that those who've not experienced it can't fully comprehend. Struggling to keep such appraisals in perspective is arguably part of the grieving process and the healing that will ultimately follow, but it is no less exacting in its toll. Fortunately, that singular, seemingly accusatory assessment was offset by countless other comments of comfort and hope—kindred expressions that once again helped us move past the darkness.

EASLEY
2009

# Chapter 7
## Traveling a Different Road

In the weeks and months that followed this third loss, we took some much-needed time to regroup and to absorb as much as we could, all that had happened, giving ourselves an opportunity to grieve and recover. Four years had passed since we began our efforts to have a child. While our friends were parenting preschoolers or experiencing subsequent pregnancies, we worked to reconcile our grief.

At Roger's suggestion, we joined a wonderful bereavement group, The Compassionate Friends. It was comprised of people who experienced grief through loss with particular emphasis on the death of a child. It provided a great deal of comfort for us and, I believe, helped us to move beyond the sorrow to focus on what we had together as well as on the promise of what was yet to come. It was not long after beginning our participation in the group that we made the decision to begin the process to adopt a baby.

In the mid-eighties, Catholic Family Services (CFS) was the primary resource for infant adoption. Rarely in those days did one read an ad in the classifieds of prospective parents longingly seeking to provide a loving home to an infant, or of an individual seeking a caring adoptive couple for a baby who, for whatever reasons, could not be raised by the birth parent.

As should be the case, the procedures for qualifying for adoption were extensive and protracted. It involved an in-depth analysis of every aspect of our lives. Physical health, mental status, financial capability, and virtually every other dimension of experience, both personal and professional, were addressed, examined, and judged. It occurred to us, as it no doubt has to countless other prospective parents going through the rigorous adoption regimen that if a similar vetting process were undertaken with every pregnancy, the world, and certainly numerous children, would be far better off.

After a grueling case study, a physical examination of our home and completion of reams of paperwork, we were approved for infant adoption and placed on a waiting list that we were told was quite long. Practically on a whim, we decided to talk with the social services department in our locality to determine if there might be any hope of adoption through them. It seemed worth the effort given the probable extended period before a baby might come available through Catholic Family Services. The social worker in charge of family issues greeted us warmly. She patiently listened to our story and our revelation that we had completed the application process for CFS, and that we were on their waiting list. While she was very empathic and genuinely seemed to want to help us, she relayed that no babies had ever been given up for adoption in our area; nevertheless, she would certainly keep our file on hand. We parted ways disappointed but grateful that we at least had the opportunity to share our story and convey our hopes, should the situation in the county change.

We moved back into a regular routine: jobs, weekends, winter moving into spring. As so often happens in life, a single moment changes everything. I came home from work shortly before Bruce on a March afternoon in 1986. I saw we had a message on the answering machine, and routinely pushed the button to hear it. What came next was the voice of the county social worker that we'd met a few months before. She related with both surprise and excitement that they had a four-week-old, red-haired baby boy for us and asked that we contact her immediately. That Bruce too, was a redhead, that the county had never had a baby up for adoption before, that despite months of paperwork and other extensive qualifying steps with CFS, a baby was available from a different source, seemed inconceivable. Even more astonishing, the county could use the qualifying steps already taken to begin the adoption process. All this made that spring afternoon telephone call nothing short of incredible.

We had a miracle—a healthy, wonderful, redheaded baby boy, and our joy could not be adequately expressed. We were told as much as confidentiality would allow. The baby's mother was twenty-four years old and had made the decision to give up her son only after a great deal of careful, painful consideration. The birth father had denied paternity and terminated the relationship, and she wanted a much better life for her baby than she believed she could provide for him by herself. She had apparently approached the county social service department about the adoption only a short time after our initial contact. In this extraordinary act of unselfish love for a child she might never know, two complete strangers would forever hold for her a lifetime of gratitude and an indescribable kinship.

Bruce and I were overjoyed and overwhelmed. Suddenly, we were going to be parents, and although we'd been through all the lead-up experiences of the past, the stark reality that it was now upon us was both exciting and daunting.

Fortunately, legalities provided some measure of assistance. It was required that the birth father be given twenty-five days to state or deny his claim to paternity before any steps toward adoption could be taken. This period occurred in the baby's first four weeks of life and had to be substantiated before we could even be made aware of the possibility of adoption. Following this, another four-week period was required to afford the birth mother the option to change her mind. However, during this time, we were allowed to see the baby at the home of the foster parents as often as both sets of schedules would allow.

Sandi and Steve were a wonderful, extraordinary couple. Had we been given the choice ourselves, we could not have chosen any two people better suited to be foster parents to our son. Their warmth and loving care for him coupled with their open arms and genuine acceptance of Bruce and me into their home and into their lives, laid the foundation for a cherished friendship and a special bond.

So, for every night of that four-week period, we spent time with our new son getting to know him, learning his likes and his habits, stepping tentatively into new parenthood, and finally realizing, through this extraordinary turn of events, the realization of the dream that had eluded us for six years and countless days of grief and loss.

Adoption is defined as taking another into a relationship and by choice, making him or her one's own. In reality, it is this and so much more. For us it was a profound gift—the result of an extraordinary decision of love and selflessness on the part of a young woman who felt she could not give her child the life she had hoped for him to have. On April 10, 1986, we took our eight-week-old son Michael from the county courthouse to his new home and began our life together as a family.

EASLEY
2009

# Chapter 8
# Parenthood

It was never more evident than in those initial days that there is a meaningful reason for the nine-month period that enables a gradual evolution into the role and substance of parenthood. True, we'd already experienced the early phases of that preparation, but the actual reality of the situation—the baby, the sleepless nights and his hours of disconsolate crying, the worries, and the anxiety that followed—blurred any sense of confidence we might have otherwise acquired. Nevertheless, like most first-time parents and their infants, the three of us gradually worked our way into a routine that softened and smoothed the rough edges.

Too, there were those crazy twenty-twenty hindsight moments that a second child never experiences. The nights when we laid with Mike on one or the other of our chests until he fell asleep, and then as though walking on an egg-laden path, we carried him almost without movement, to his crib, gingerly laid him down, dropped to our knees, and crawled out of the room. We held our breath in the hope that he wouldn't wake up and require the entire scenario be reenacted once again. This went on for several months until finally we decided to follow Mom's advice and let him cry. As long as we knew he was fed, dry, and not in pain, there was no legitimate reason for jumping to his disposal at all hours of the night. It only took one long, agonizing, guilt-ridden, three-hour period to break the pattern, but it worked and another of many, many milestones had been achieved.

Mike was an adorable little baby. He honestly looked so much like Bruce. Their hair color and skin-tone matched so well that few people could believe he was adopted. We could not imagine then, nor can we to this day, loving Mike any more if he had been born to us. He was our miracle baby, the answer to a thousand prayers, and the realization of a dream that had eluded us not only in time, but also in incalculable sorrow. He filled our lives and truly made us whole. Adoption had given us what nature could not. This little red-haired boy was the source of immeasurable joy and fulfillment after such a long period of empty, wrenching loss.

# Chapter 9
## Against the Odds

Those early years went by quickly, and when Mike turned three, we began to think about having another baby. We felt strongly that we didn't want him to be an only child. As one of four, I was very close to my siblings and couldn't imagine my life without them. I wanted the same experience, at least with one sister or brother, for our son. I was thirty-nine then, and to express that my proverbial biological clock was ticking, was, especially in my case, an extraordinary understatement. We knew the challenges that faced us with another pregnancy, and the age issue with adoption was looming significantly as well.

We decided to consult with Roger, and if we received his blessing, we would pursue pregnancy one last time. He endorsed our efforts with the caveat that if we were successful in achieving the pregnancy, there would be an entirely different approach this time.

Thus, the fertility regimen began anew. Maybe it was for practicality or realism, or maybe it was to provide ourselves with an out, but we made a pact with each other that if I didn't get pregnant by my fortieth birthday (pregnancy dotage in its own right!) then we would accept the situation, continue to be very grateful for the cherished little boy we had, and move on with our lives.

I began taking Clomid right away. Once again, we were hostage to the basal thermometer, the cycles of nature, and the gravity-defying contortions. Add to that mix the needs and demands of an active three-year-old and the concepts of making love and intimacy took on entirely new meanings!

Month after month went by without success. We'd been trying since February and into the spring, summer, and early fall. We had begun to steel ourselves to the probability that Mike would be our only child. Bruce had been born late in his parents' lives. He had two older sisters who were twenty-two and twenty-five years older than he was. He lost his mother at thirteen, and his only sustaining memories of his childhood with his older parent were those of a tumultuous relationship with a man who was much more like his grandfather than his father. We would not alter our commitment to accept whatever reality faced us when I turned forty in late January.

It seems so typical of life that just when you're pretty certain you've got a handle on which way it's going to turn, it jags to the right or left, taking you along a path you didn't expect or thought too unlikely to pursue. Our curve, much to our great joy, came almost exactly two months to the day before my fortieth birthday. Roger confirmed that I was pregnant just before Thanksgiving, making the due date in early July. I decided to relay the news to Bruce by placing on the cupboard, a flyer on nursing I'd grabbed from Roger's office. When he got home from work that night, after the usual conversation he noticed it, looked at my face, and for one final time, together with our son, the journey had begun again.

Roger was true to his word. I could maintain a generally normal routine for the first trimester, caring for Mike, working, and enjoying family activities. However, if we made it successfully through the always-tentative initial three months, *I would be placed on complete bed rest for the remaining six months of the pregnancy!*

Even in light of all we'd been through, I was really taken back by the thought of remaining in bed or on the couch, unable to do anything but shower and go to the bathroom for six months, especially with an almost four-year-old child. How would we do it? What kinds of unbelievable demands would it place on Bruce? Could I, could we, possibly deal with those kinds of constraints with the ever-looming possibility that it might all come to the same unbearable end?

The significant milestone of the completion of the first trimester arrived. At that juncture, Roger scheduled me for a "womb renovation." My cervix would once again, essentially be surgically tied shut, a step taken to ensure that in the event of another natural failure, the cervix would be prevented from opening and initiating premature labor. In addition, I would start on a daily regimen of an anti-labor medication. These steps, coupled with the complete inactivity would be our triple-pronged defense against all the known forces that had defeated our efforts in the past.

It's amazing what can be done when singly and together a commitment is made to face whatever comes, putting one foot in front of the other, and staying focused on the goal. To assert that Bruce stepped up to the plate would be an immeasurable understatement. Once we reached the start of the second trimester and the defensive approach was put into place, he took over every responsibility involved in caring for Mike: getting him to and from preschool and the sitter, cooking meals, cleaning the house, and addressing the countless other commitments and responsibilities that come with the daily routine of family life, all while holding a full-time job.

If anyone had ever told me I would spend six months of my life essentially sitting down in a recliner or lying in a bed, changing venues only to eat, shower, or answer the call of nature, I would have told them it wouldn't be possible. But that would have been before the losses, before the joy of a child in our lives, and the awareness of what a sibling would mean to him. That would have been before the hope that comes with new methods to address old failings, and that would have been before we knew that we had only one final chance.

After all of our experiences, and especially with the new
dimension that now existed in the endless hours to focus on
the past, every step in the process became another milestone.
I was on a weekly office routine with Roger, and each one
successfully completed was another week behind us.

At sixteen weeks, a major event loomed. Given my age and
the high-risk nature of my pregnancy, it was recommended
that I undergo amniocentesis. The procedure would rule out
(or confirm) a variety of possible problems associated with
later pregnancies and would provide a very accurate gauge of
the baby's health. It would also relate, if we chose to know,
the baby's gender. We anticipated the event with very mixed
feelings. What if, after all we'd been through, something was
seriously wrong with the baby? What if something, anything,
didn't look right at this stage of the pregnancy? How would
we deal with a potential loss that had a totally different basis?
It would be very easy to drive ourselves crazy with this kind
of speculation, so we decided to wait to cross any bridges that
might present themselves until and only if, they did.

The amniocentesis proceeded without any problems and
the outcome was wonderful: no problems with the baby, no
concerns with the pregnancy at this stage, and we were to be
the proud parents of another son. I remember hoping early
on that the baby would be a girl, since it would be terrific to
have one of each, but even more, because I thought it would
make Mike feel particularly special if he were the only son.
However, it didn't take but a nanosecond to remove that

concern. Mike, Bruce, and I were all thrilled at the prospect of a new baby brother and the joy—the unfamiliar normalcy of that revelation—was an extraordinary moment for Bruce and I that helped to move us forward with renewed hope.

By now, the baby's activity had become an ongoing and cherished reality. Mike would place his little hands on my stomach and smile when he felt his little brother move. For Bruce and me, it served always as a manifestation of a complex mix of anxiety and hope, anticipation and fear. Reaching the next monumental milestone, passing the seven-month mark, could not come soon enough. If we could overcome the terrible chronological benchmark that had taken two of our babies from us then we might just make it—and make it we did! Although we were certainly not there yet, we were realizing progress, and with each visit to Roger and each confirmation that things were proceeding as they should, our hope grew more substantial.

Finally, we found ourselves at the start of the ninth month, a homestretch of sorts. As a kind of confirmation of his own growing confidence, Roger began to lay out the plans and process for the birth. The baby would have to be delivered by Cesarean section, both because of my prior C-sections and the uterine reconstruction. The natural birth process could create a significant risk of rupture, a complication we certainly didn't need. The delivery date was set for July 6. I would remain on the anti-labor medication until the Fourth of July, when I would be allowed to come off bed rest for the two days prior to the baby's birth. Talk about Independence Day!

At long, long last, the Fourth of July 1990 arrived! It was a beautiful day and we'd been invited to a pool party and cookout at the home of friends who had the celebration every year. Mom had come from Maine to be here for the delivery and came to the gathering with us. Mike was thrilled at the chance to go swimming with Dad and the slew of other kids in the pool, and I was basking in the unbelievable experience of being outside without having to worry about moving around too much. We were finally at the point where, if I were to go into labor, the baby was ready to make a healthy, fully developed entrance into the world. For the first time in nine months—in ten years—I felt a kind of normalcy that I had never known in pregnancy before, and it was fantastic. That Fourth of July was an extraordinary day in so many ways and one I will remember always.

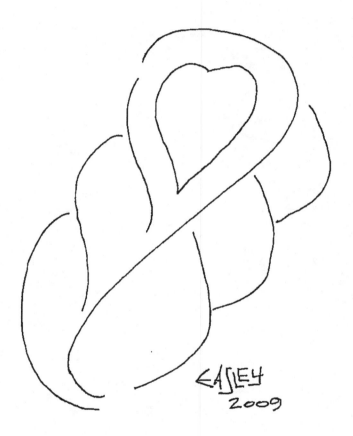

EASLEY
2009

# Chapter 10
## So Much for Schedules, Mom and Dad!

We stayed at the gathering into the early evening. Mike and Bruce enjoyed the pool immensely, and Mom and I, along with so many friends, reveled in the freedom of my new status and in the anticipation of the baby's delivery in just two days!

When we returned home that evening, I was busy mentally planning the last-minute things I would put into place the next day. Arrangements had been made for Mike to stay with his beloved babysitter, Sharon, and the nursery was ready to receive its much-anticipated new resident. I had a bag packed with clothes and Bruce had arranged to be off work. The one important task I wanted very much to accomplish was to write notes of love and appreciation to both Bruce and Mom for their unceasing support and love through the extraordinary nine months we were about to complete and for sharing in all the circumstances, all the sorrow, and all the joy that had comprised the past ten years of our lives. It momentarily brought to mind the thought that maybe it's a very good thing we can't see into the future, especially in the short term, for we might decide to opt out if given the choice, and in doing so, possibly miss out on some of life's most extraordinary gifts!

Everyone was ready for a good night's rest after the day's celebration. Mike fell asleep quickly and so did we. Tomorrow would be the last full day of the only successful pregnancy I'd had. It would mark an extraordinary milestone and would no doubt be filled with anxious, but exhilarating anticipation of what was to come on the sixth.

Well, so much for the best-laid plans of mice, men, obstetricians, and parents! At around five o'clock, I awoke with what were unquestionably, regular labor pains. By the time I got myself to the bathroom, my water had broken and our little guy was making it glaringly clear that he had his own schedule.

We immediately called Roger who obviously instructed us to get to the hospital as quickly as possible. Bruce rushed to take Mike to the sitter just a few streets away. Mom helped me as much as she could and then hurried to get herself ready. No doubt due to the stress of the unexpected events that were unfolding, she became sick to her stomach. Bruce returned and helped me pull together the few things I'd set aside to take with me. We called my best friend, Donna and my dear cousin, Susan, both of whom, along with Mom, wanted to be present for the delivery. Unbelievably, I remembered to grab a box of blank cards and a pen so I could attempt to write during the ride to the hospital, the notes to Bruce and Mom that I'd planned to leisurely complete that day.

Mom finally felt well enough (or knew she had to be, whether she did or not!) to grab a few of her things, and we were on our way to one of the most extraordinary destinations of our lives. The trip seemed to take forever. I remember writing the notes between labor pains, all the while thinking that our own little firecracker already had a mind of his own—just like his big brother!

In looking back later, I was struck by how extraordinarily successful the anti-labor medication had been. It had prevented what I was experiencing now, just hours after Roger had instructed that I stop taking it. We'd come a long way since the loss of our first son more than nine years before, and it had made all the difference.

We arrived at the hospital and I was rushed to the labor and delivery ward. Although I'd been experiencing contractions for a few hours by this time, I hadn't dilated at all, so the decision was made to hold off on the C-section for a while to see what developed. To this day, I'm not sure why the decision to wait was made, as it was already certain that I was going to deliver the baby surgically. The ordeal of true extended labor, while an event I'd longed to experience many times in the past, was not one I was at all excited about enduring on this day, especially if I wasn't going to deliver vaginally. Finally, after about two and a half hours and some muted concerns about the baby's heart rate, I was brought to the operating room and prepped for the delivery. Bruce was again beside me every step of the way, and just on the other side of the window and within view of the entire procedure, were Mom, Donna, and Susan.

I was given an epidural and again laid out on the table with arms spread wide and a cloth blocking my view of the surgery. Bruce relayed what was happening at every step, while Roger reassured both of us that everything was going well.

# Chapter 11
# We Have Another Miracle!

At long, long last, early on the morning of July 5, 1990, Eric, was born—healthy, whole, alive! The indescribable joy and overwhelming emotion of succeeding in giving birth was finally ours. His cry, and ultimately, his little body resting on my chest, confirmed the realization of the dream that had eluded us for almost a decade. We had another miracle: we had another son, and against all the odds, our family was now complete.

Eric, like his brother, Mike, has brought a unique and indescribable joy to our family. He is a thoughtful, sensitive, and insightful young man with a wonderful sense of humor and a heart filled with compassion.

\* \* \*

Even as I write this memoir, almost nineteen years after Eric's birth, I am still overwhelmed at the unbelievable course of events that brought each of our sons to us, and before them, our first three children who passed away. The invulnerability and the sense of insulation from the vagaries of life that come with youth left us very early in our quest to become parents. We were blindsided by the unforeseen loss of our first son and were certain we had bested the dictates of fate in the pregnancies that would have brought us our daughters—we had not.

Perhaps it's my enduring need to view the glass as half full instead of half empty, or just a simplistic way of dealing with circumstances much larger than ourselves, and over which we have no control, but the only perspective I have ever been able to put on those heartbreaking losses, is two-fold:

We have much to look forward to at our deaths when we will meet and substantiate our love for our three lost children.

No door closes that does not yield to the opening of another: we would not have the sons we love and cherish in our lives here and now if we had not experienced those losses—however unbearable they were and will always be.

It is a simplistic, arguably childish way of viewing a wrenching course of events, but I guess we each find our own mechanisms and sources of healing. This, and the joy of these two extraordinary young men, and their father—unquestionably the loves of my life—have made the journey not only bearable, but also immeasurably rewarding.

# Epilogue

Today, our sons are finding their own way. Mike is a paratrooper in the army, and Eric has just completed his first year in college. They are a constant source of joy and pride for Bruce and me and are without doubt the most cherished gifts of our lives. When we began our journey so many years ago, we couldn't have foreseen the paths we would have to walk or the pitfalls that lay within them. The losses were the darkest, most difficult times either of us had ever known, but somehow, in the love we had for each other, the unceasing support we were constantly given by family and friends, and in Roger and Dan's willingness to guide us through whatever we had to face, we emerged with the miracles that are our sons.

If there is a single message in all this that I would hope to provide to anyone reading our story or sadly, sharing in some or all of its events, it would be to stay the course—if that course is right for you. No one can define that for someone else, and no one can calculate for another how much is enough, or what measure of sorrow and loss constitutes a breaking point. I can only tell you that I believe, as trite as it may seem, that everything happens for a purpose.

Obstetrical medical science has come an extraordinary distance in the years since we began our quest to have children. Babies are now surviving and thriving at unbelievably small birth weights. Neonatal intensive care has an expansive arsenal of drugs, technology, equipment, and knowledge that was unimaginable during my childbearing years. Nevertheless, those incalculable, soul-wrenching losses continue to occur today and their victims are still compelled to bear not only the heartbreak of the event, but the onslaught of well-meaning, often patently insensitive statements, aimed at comforting, but that succeed only in hurting.

Pregnancy loss, no matter what the circumstance, is an agony singular in its impact and breadth. An extremely personal grief that mourns not only the child who will not be brought to life, but also the roles, that in that individual case, will never be realized. It is the theft of past, present, and future and the demise of a whole construct of life that can never be completely duplicated, regardless of whether successful pregnancies or adoptions follow. Nevertheless, subsequent pregnancies and/or adoptions provide a new realization of promise, each bringing its own unique joy and fulfillment.

Thank you for taking the time to share our story. I can only hope that our experience has provided some measure of promise, encouragement, and kinship. Though Bruce and I would never have chosen the course that was ours to take, we are so grateful for its ultimate outcome. The individual miracles that are our sons have given to us our most cherished gifts, and we are grateful beyond measure for them.

Jayne H. Easley
May 2009

# Resources

## Infertility

The National Infertility Association
www.resolve.org/

Web MD Infertility Center
www.webmd.com/infertility-and-reproduction/

Infertility and Surrogacy—Resources and Information
www.babyzone.com/preconception/infertility

Infertility Tips, Articles, and Resources
www.abcinfertility.com/

# Pregnancy Loss and Grief

The Compassionate Friends. An organization focused on dealing with grief in the loss of a child.
P.O. Box 3696
Oak Brook, Illinois 60522
Bereaved Parents of the USA
P.O. Box 95
Park Forest, Illinois 60466

HAND—Help After Neonatal Death
P.O. Box 341
Las Gatos, California 95031

Remembering Our Babies—Pregnancy Loss Support
www.october15th.com

OBGYN.net Women's Health: Loss and Bereavement
www.obgyn.net/women/loss/loss.htm

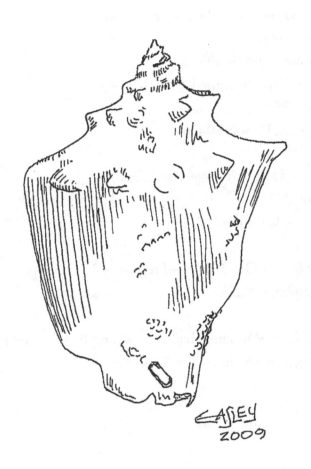

CASLEY
2009

# Adoption

*Adopting: Sound Choices, Strong Families*
Patricia Irwin Johnston

*Adoption in the United States: A Reference for Families,*
*Professionals, and Students*
Martha J. Henry and Daniel Pollack

Adoption Services
www.AdoptionNetwork.com

National Council for Adoption ( NCFA) Adoption Resources
www.adoptioncouncil.org/

Adoption in the United States
www.AmericanAdoptions.com

Adoption Information Resources
www.Websites.adoption.com

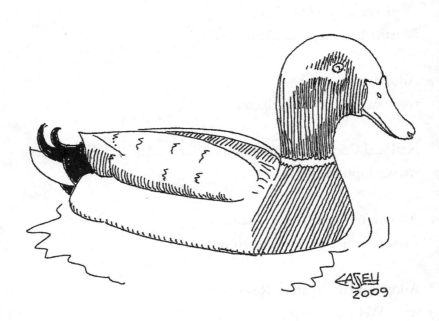

# High Risk Pregnancy

*Manual of High Risk Pregnancy and Delivery*
Elizabeth S. Gilbert

*Management of High-Risk Pregnancy*
John T. Queenan

High Risk Pregnancy
www.obfocus.com/

High Risk Situations and Complications in Pregnancy,
Labor, and Birth
www.moonlily.com/obc/complications.html/

*The High Risk Pregnancy Sourcebook*
www.amazon.com/HighRiskPregnancySourcebook

The High Risk Support Center
www.thesurvivorsclub.org/support-center/health/womens-health/
high-risk-pregnancy.html

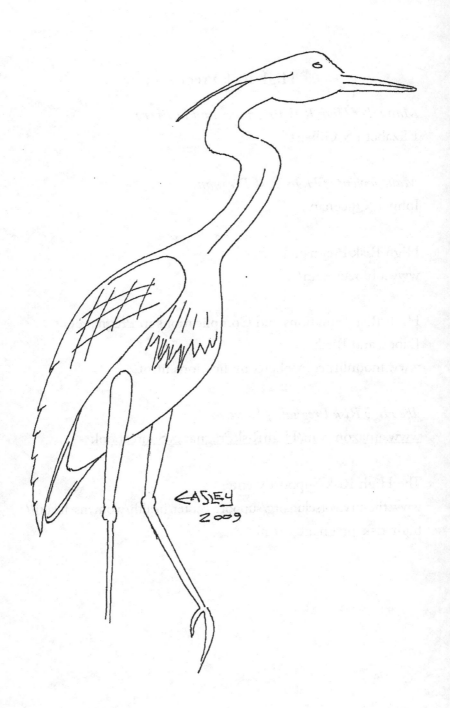

Printed in the United States
by Baker & Taylor Publisher Services